"'Kalashnikov,"
he said curtly.
"Sub-machine-gun.
Gas operated.
Thirty rounds in 7.62
millimetre. Favourite
with the KGB'"

IAN FLEMING
Born 28 May 1908, London
Died 12 August 1964, Canterbury

'The Living Daylights' first published in book form in
Octopussy and The Living Daylights in 1966; 'From a View
to a Kill' first published in book form in *For Your Eyes Only*
in 1960.

ALSO PUBLISHED BY PENGUIN BOOKS
*Casino Royale · Live and Let Die · Moonraker · Diamonds Are
Forever · From Russia with Love · Dr No · Goldfinger · For Your
Eyes Only · Thunderball · The Spy Who Loved Me · On Her
Majesty's Secret Service · You Only Live Twice · The Man with
the Golden Gun · Octopussy and The Living Daylights ·
Quantum of Solace: The Complete James Bond Short Stories*

IAN FLEMING

The Living Daylights

PENGUIN BOOKS

PENGUIN CLASSICS

Published by the Penguin Group
Penguin Books Ltd, 80 Strand, London WC2R ORL, England
Penguin Group (USA) Inc., 375 Hudson Street, New York, New York 10014, USA
Penguin Group (Canada), 90 Eglinton Avenue East, Suite 700, Toronto, Ontario,
Canada M4P 2Y3 (a division of Pearson Penguin Canada Inc.)
Penguin Ireland, 25 St Stephen's Green, Dublin 2, Ireland (a division of Penguin Books Ltd)
Penguin Group (Australia), 250 Camberwell Road, Camberwell, Victoria 3124, Australia
(a division of Pearson Australia Group Pty Ltd)
Penguin Books India Pvt Ltd, 11 Community Centre, Panchsheel Park,
New Delhi – 110 017, India
Penguin Group (NZ), 67 Apollo Drive, Rosedale, North Shore 0632, New Zealand
(a division of Pearson New Zealand Ltd)
Penguin Books (South Africa) (Pty) Ltd, 24 Sturdee Avenue, Rosebank, Johannesburg 2196,
South Africa

Penguin Books Ltd, Registered Offices: 80 Strand, London WC2R ORL, England

www.penguin.com

'The Living Daylights' taken from *Octopussy and The Living Daylights* published in
Penguin Classics 2006
'From a View to a Kill' taken from *For Your Eyes Only* published in Penguin Classics 2006
This edition published in Penguin Classics 2011

1

Typeset by Jouve (UK), Milton Keynes
Printed in England by Clays Ltd, St Ives plc

ISBN: 978-0-141-19597-1

www.greenpenguin.co.uk

Penguin Books is committed to a sustainable future
for our business, our readers and our planet.
The book in your hands is made from paper
certified by the Forest Stewardship Council.

Contents

The Living Daylights

James Bond lay at the five-hundred-yard firing point of the famous Century Range at Bisley. The white peg in the grass beside him said 4.4 and the same number was repeated high up on the distant butt above the single six-foot-square target that, to the human eye and in the late summer dusk, looked no larger than a postage stamp. But Bond's lens, an infra-red Sniperscope fixed above his rifle, covered the whole canvas. He could even clearly distinguish the pale-blue and beige colours into which the target was divided, and the six-inch semi-circular bull looked as big as the half moon that was already beginning to show low down in the darkening sky above the distant crest of Chobham Ridges.

James Bond's last shot had been an inner left – not good enough. He took another glance at the yellow-and-blue wind flags. They were streaming across range from the east rather more stiffly than when he had begun his shoot half an hour before, and he set two clicks more to the right on the wind gauge and traversed the cross-wires on the Sniperscope back to the point of aim. Then he settled himself, put his trigger finger gently inside the guard and on to the curve of the trigger, shallowed his breathing and very, very softly squeezed.

The vicious crack of the shot boomed across the empty range. The target disappeared below ground and at once the 'dummy' came up in its place. Yes, the black panel was in the bottom right-hand corner this time, not in the bottom left: a bull.

'Good,' said the voice of the Chief Range Officer from behind and above him. 'Stay with it.'

The target was already up again and Bond put his cheek back to its warm patch on the chunky wooden stock and his eye to the rubber eyepiece of the 'scope. He wiped his gun hand down the side of his trousers and took the pistol grip that jutted sharply down below the trigger guard. He splayed his legs an inch more. Now there were to be five rounds rapid. It would be interesting to see if that would produce 'fade'. He guessed not. This extraordinary weapon the Armourer had somehow got his hands on gave one the feeling that a standing man at a mile would be easy meat. It was mostly a .308 calibre International Experimental Target rifle built by Winchester to help American marksmen at World Championships, and it had the usual gadgets of super-accurate target weapons – a curled aluminium 'hand' at the back of the butt that extended under the armpit and held the stock firmly into the shoulder, and an adjustable pinion below the rifle's centre of gravity to allow the stock to be 'nailed' into its grooved wooden rest. The Armourer had had the usual single-shot bolt action replaced by a five-shot magazine, and he had assured Bond that if he would allow only two seconds between shots to steady the weapon there would be no fade even at five hundred yards. For the job that Bond had to do, he guessed that two seconds might be a dangerous loss of time if he missed with his first shot. Anyway, M had said that the range would be not more than three hundred yards. Bond would cut it down to one second – almost continuous fire.

'Ready?'

'Yes.'

'I'll give you a count-down from five. Now! Five, four, three, two, one. Fire!'

The ground shuddered slightly and the air sang as the five whirling scraps of cupro-nickel spat off into the dusk. The target went down and quickly rose again decorated with four small white discs closely grouped on the bull. There was no fifth disc – not even a black one to show an inner or an outer.

'The last round was low,' said the Range Officer

lowering his night-glasses. 'Thanks for the contribution. We sift the sand on those butts at the end of every year. Never get less than fifteen tons of good lead and copper scrap out of them. Good money.'

Bond had got to his feet. Corporal Menzies from the Armourers' section appeared from the pavilion of the Gun Club and knelt down to dismantle the Winchester and its rest. He looked up at Bond. He said with a hint of criticism, 'You were taking it a bit fast, sir. Last round was bound to jump wide.'

'I know, Corporal. I wanted to see how fast I *could* take it. I'm not blaming the weapon. It's the hell of a fine job. Please tell the Armourer so from me. Now I'd better get moving. You're finding your own way back to London, aren't you?'

'Yes. Good night, sir.'

The Chief Range Officer handed Bond a record of his shoot – two sighting shots and then ten rounds at each hundred yards up to five hundred. 'Damned good firing with this visibility. You ought to come back next year and have a bash at the Queen's Prize. It's open to all comers nowadays – British Commonwealth, that is.'

'Thanks. Trouble is, I'm not all that much in England. And thanks for spotting for me.' Bond glanced at the distant Clock Tower. On either side, the red danger flag and the red signal drum were coming down to show that firing had ceased. The hands stood at nine fifteen. 'I'd like to have bought you a drink, but I've got an appointment in London. Can we hold it over until that Queen's Prize you were talking about?'

The Range Officer nodded noncommittally. He had been looking forward to finding out more about this man who had appeared out of the blue after a flurry of signals from the Ministry of Defence and had then proceeded to score well over ninety per cent at all distances, and that after the range was closed for the night and visibility was poor to bad. And why had he, who only officiated at the annual July meeting, been ordered to be present? And why had he been told to see that Bond had a six-inch bull at 500 instead of the regulation fifteen-inch? And why this flummery with the danger flag and signal drum that were only used on ceremonial occasions? To put pressure on the man? To give an edge of urgency to the shoot? Bond. Commander James Bond. The NRA would surely have a record of anyone who could shoot like that. He'd remember to give them a call. Funny time to have an appointment in London. Probably a girl. The Range Officer's undistinguished face assumed a disgruntled expression. Sort of fellow who got all the girls he wanted.

The two men walked through the handsome façade of Club Row behind the range to Bond's car that stood opposite the bullet-pitted iron reproduction of Landseer's famous 'Running Deer'. 'Nice-looking job,' commented the Range Officer. 'Never seen a body like that on a Continental. Have it made specially?'

'Yes. The Sports Saloons are really only two-seaters. And damned little luggage space. So I got Mulliner's to make it into a real two-seater with plenty of boot. Selfish car, I'm afraid. Well, good night. And thanks again.' The exhaust boomed healthily and the back wheels briefly spat gravel.

The Chief Range Officer watched the ruby lights vanish up King's Avenue towards the London road. He turned on his heel and went to find Corporal Menzies on a search for information that was to prove fruitless. The corporal remained as wooden as the big mahogany box he was in the process of loading into a khaki Land-Rover without military symbols. The Range Officer was a major. He tried pulling his rank without success. The Land-Rover hammered away in Bond's wake. The major walked moodily off to the offices of the National Rifle Association to try and find out what he wanted in the library under 'Bond, J.'.

James Bond's appointment was not with a girl. It was with a BEA flight to Hanover and Berlin. As he bit off the miles to London Airport, pushing the big car hard so as to have plenty of time for a drink, three drinks, before the take off, only part of his mind was on the road. The rest was re-examining, for the umpteenth time, the sequence that was now leading him to an appointment with an aeroplane. But only an interim appointment. His final rendezvous on one of the next three nights in Berlin was with a man. He had to see this man and infallibly shoot him dead.

When, at around two thirty that afternoon, James Bond had gone in through the double-padded doors and had sat down opposite the turned-away profile on the other side of the big desk, he had sensed trouble. There was no greeting. M's head was sunk into his stiff turned-down collar in a Churchillian pose of gloomy reflection, and there was a droop of bitterness at the corners of his lips. He swivelled his chair round to face Bond, gave him an appraising glance as if, Bond thought, to see that his tie was straight and his hair properly brushed, and then began speaking, fast, clipping off his sentences as if he wanted to be rid of what he was saying, and of Bond, as quickly as possible.

'Number 272. He's a good man. You won't have come across him. Simple reason that he's been holed up in Novaya Zemlya since the war. Now he's trying to get out – loaded with stuff. Atomic and rockets. And their plan for whole new series of tests. For 1961. To put the heat on the West. Something to do with Berlin. Don't quite get the picture but the FO say if it's true it's terrific. Makes nonsense of the Geneva Conference and all this blether about nuclear disarmament the Communist bloc are putting out. He's got as far as East Berlin. But he's got practically the whole of the KGB on his tail – and the East German security forces of course. He's holed up somewhere in the city and he got one message over to us – that he'd be coming across between six and seven pm on one of the next three nights – tomorrow, next day, or the day after. He gave the crossing point. Trouble is,' the downward curve of M's lips became even more bitter, 'the courier he used was a double. Station WB bowled him out yesterday. Quite by chance. Had a lucky break with one of the KGB codes. The courier'll be flown out for trial, of course. But that won't help. The KGB know that 272 will be making a run for it. They know when. They know where. They know just as much as we do and no more. Now, the code we cracked was a one-day-only setting on their machines. But we got the whole of that day's traffic and that was good enough. They plan to shoot him on the run. At this street crossing between East and West Berlin he gave us in his message. They're mounting quite an operation – operation "Extase" they call it. Put their best sniper on the job. All we know about him is that his

code name is the Russian for "Trigger". Station WB
guess he's the same man they've used before for sniper
work. Long-range stuff across the frontier. He's going
to be guarding this crossing every night and his job is
to get 272. Of course they'd obviously prefer to do a
smoother job with machine-guns and what have you.
But it's quiet in Berlin at the moment and apparently
the word is it's got to stay so. Anyway, ' M shrugged,
'they've got confidence in this "Trigger" operator and
that's the way it's going to be!'

'Where do I come in, sir?' James Bond had guessed
the answer, guessed why M was showing his dislike of
the whole business. This was going to be dirty work
and Bond, because he belonged to the Double-O Section, had been chosen for it. Perversely, Bond wanted to
force M to put it in black and white. This was going to
be bad news, dirty news, and he didn't want to hear it
from one of the Section officers, or even from the Chief
of Staff. This was to be murder. All right. Let M bloody
well say so.

'Where do you come in, 007?' M looked coldly across
the desk. 'You know where you come in. You've got to
kill this sniper. And you've got to kill him before he gets
272. That's all. Is that understood?' The clear blue eyes
remained cold as ice. But Bond knew that they remained
so only with an effort of will. M didn't like sending any

man to a killing. But, when it had to be done, he always put on this fierce, cold act of command. Bond knew why. It was to take some of the pressure, some of the guilt, off the killer's shoulders.

So now Bond, who knew these things, decided to make it easy and quick for M. He got to his feet. 'That's all right, sir. I suppose the Chief of Staff has got all the gen. I'd better go and put in some practice. It wouldn't do to miss.' He walked to the door.

M said quietly, 'Sorry to have to hand this to you. Nasty job. But it's got to be done well.'

'I'll do my best, sir.' James Bond walked out and closed the door behind him. He didn't like the job, but on the whole he'd rather have it himself than have the responsibility of ordering someone else to go and do it.

The Chief of Staff had been only a shade more sympathetic. 'Sorry you've bought this one, James,' he had said. 'But Tanqueray was definite that he hadn't got anyone good enough on his Station, and this isn't the sort of job you can ask a regular soldier to do. Plenty of top marksmen in the BAOR, but a live target needs another kind of nerve. Anyway, I've been on to Bisley and fixed a shoot for you tonight at eight fifteen when the ranges will be closed. Visibility should be about the same as you'll be getting in Berlin around an hour earlier. The Armourer's got the gun – a real target job, and he's sending it down with one of his men. You'll find your own way. Then you're booked on a midnight BEA charter flight to Berlin. Take a taxi to this address.' He handed Bond a piece of paper. 'Go up to the fourth floor and you'll find Tanqueray's Number 2 waiting for you. Then I'm afraid you'll just have to sit it out for the next three days.'

'How about the gun? Am I supposed to take it through the German customs in a golf bag or something?'

The Chief of Staff hadn't been amused. 'It'll go over in the FO bag. You'll have it by tomorrow midday.' He had reached for a signal pad. 'Well, you'd better get cracking. I'll just let Tanqueray know everything's fixed.'

James Bond glanced down at the dim blue face of the dashboard clock. Ten fifteen. With any luck by this time tomorrow it would all be finished. After all, it was the life of this man 'Trigger' against the life of 272. It wasn't *exactly* murder. Pretty near it, though. He gave a vicious blast on his triple windhorns at an inoffensive family saloon, took the roundabout in a quite unnecessary dry skid, wrenched the wheel harshly to correct it and pointed the nose of the Bentley towards the distant glow that was London Airport.

The ugly six-storey building at the corner of Kochstrasse and the Wilhelmstrasse was the only one standing in a waste of empty bombed space. Bond paid off his taxi and got a brief impression of waist-high weeds and half-tidied rubble walls stretching away to a big deserted crossroads lit by a central cluster of yellowish arc lamps, before he pushed the bell for the fourth floor and at once heard the click of the door opener. The door closed itself behind him and he walked over the uncarpeted cement floor to the old-fashioned lift. The smell of cabbage, cheap cigar smoke and stale sweat reminded him of other apartment houses in Germany and Central Europe. Even the sigh and faint squeal of the slow lift were part of a hundred assignments when he had been fired off by M, like a projectile, at some distant target where a problem waited for his coming, waited to be solved by him. At least this time the reception committee was on his side. This time there was nothing to fear at the top of the stairs.

Number 2 of Secret Service Station WB was a lean, tense man in his early forties. He wore the uniform of his profession – well-cut, well-used, lightweight tweeds in a dark-green herringbone, a soft white silk shirt and an old school tie – in his case Wykehamist. At the sight of the tie, and while they exchanged conventional greetings in the small musty lobby of the apartment, Bond's spirits, already low, sank another degree. He knew the type: backbone of the Civil Service; over-crammed and under-loved at Winchester; a good second in PPE at Oxford; the war, staff jobs he'would have done meticulously; perhaps an OBE; Allied Control Commission in Germany where he had been recruited into the I Branch and thence – because he was the ideal staff man and AI with Security and because he thought he would find life, drama, romance, the things he had never had – into the Secret Service. A sober, careful man had been needed to chaperon Bond on this ugly business. Captain Paul Sender, late of the Welsh Guards, had been the obvious choice. He had bought it. Now, like a good Wykehamist, he concealed his distaste for the job beneath careful, trite conversation as he showed Bond the layout of the apartment and the arrangements that had been made for the executioner's preparedness and, to a modest extent, his comfort.

The flat consisted of a large double bedroom, a bathroom, and a kitchen containing tinned food, milk, butter, eggs, tea, bacon, bread and one bottle of Dimple Haig. The only odd feature in the bedroom was that one of the double beds was angled up against the curtains covering the single broad window and was piled high with three mattresses below the bedclothes.

Captain Sender said, 'Care to have a look at the field of fire? Then I can explain what the other side have in mind.'

Bond was tired. He didn't particularly want to go to sleep with the picture of the battlefield on his mind. He said, 'That'd be fine.'

Captain Sender switched off the lights. Chinks from the street light at the intersection showed round the curtains. 'Don't want to draw the curtains,' said Captain Sender. 'Unlikely, but they may be on the look-out for a covering party for 272. If you'd just lie on the bed and get your head under the curtains, I'll brief you about what you'll be looking at. Look to the left.'

It was a sash window and the bottom half was open. The mattress, by design, gave only a little and James Bond found himself more or less in the firing position he had been in on the Century Range, but now staring across broken, thickly weeded bombed ground towards the bright river of the Zimmerstrasse – the border with East Berlin. It looked about a hundred and fifty yards away. Captain Sender's voice from above him and behind the curtain began reciting. It reminded Bond of a spiritualist séance.

'That's bombed ground in front of you. Plenty of

cover. A hundred and thirty yards of it up to the frontier. Then the frontier – the street – and then a big stretch of more bombed ground on the enemy side. That's why 272 chose this route. It's one of the few places in the town which is broken land – thick weeds, ruined walls, cellars – on both sides of the frontier. He will sneak through that mess on the other side and make a dash across the Zimmerstrasse for the mess on our side. Trouble is, he'll have thirty yards of brightly lit frontier to sprint across. That'll be the killing ground. Right?'

Bond said, 'Yes.' He said it softly. The scent of the enemy, the need to take care, already had him by the nerves.

'To your left, that big new ten-storey block is the Haus der Ministerien, the chief brain-centre of East Berlin. You can see the lights are still on in most of the windows. Most of those'll stay on all night. These chaps work hard – shifts all round the clock. You probably won't need to worry about the lighted ones. This "Trigger" chap'll almost certainly fire from one of the dark windows. You'll see there's a block of four together on the corner above the intersection. They've stayed dark last night and tonight. They've got the best field of fire. From here, their range varies from three hundred to three hundred and ten yards. I've got all the figures and so on when you want them. You needn't worry about

much else. That street stays empty during the night –
only the motorized patrols about every half an hour – light
armoured car with a couple of motor-cycles as escort.
Last night, which I suppose is typical, between six and
seven when this thing's going to be done, there were a
few people that came and went out of that side door.
Civil servant types. Before that nothing out of the
ordinary – usual flow of people in and out of a busy
government building – except, of all things, a whole
damned women's orchestra. Made the hell of a racket
in some concert hall they've got in there. Part of the
block is the Ministry of Culture. Otherwise nothing –
certainly none of the KGB people we know, nor
any signs of preparation for a job like this. But there
wouldn't be. They're careful chaps, the opposition.
Anyway, have a good look. Don't forget it's darker than
it will be tomorrow around six. But you can get the general picture.'

Bond got the general picture and it stayed with him
long after the other man was asleep and snoring softly
with a gentle regular clicking sound – a Wykehamist
snore, Bond reflected irritably.

Yes, he had got the picture – the picture of a flicker
of movement among the shadowy ruins on the other
side of the gleaming river of light, a pause, then the
wild zigzagging sprint of a man in the full glare of the

arcs, the crash of gunfire and either a crumpled, sprawling heap in the middle of the wide street or the noise of his onward dash through the weeds and rubble of the Western Sector – sudden death or a home run. The true gauntlet! How much time would Bond have to spot the Russian sniper in one of those dark windows? And kill him? Five seconds? Ten? When dawn edged the curtains with gun-metal, Bond capitulated to his fretting mind. It had won. He went softly into the bathroom and surveyed the ranks of medicine bottles that a thoughtful Secret Service had provided to keep its executioner in good shape. He selected the Tuinal, chased down two of the ruby-and-blue depth-charges with a glass of water and went back to bed. Then, pole-axed, he slept.

He awoke at midday. The flat was empty. Bond drew the curtains to let in the grey Prussian day and, standing well back from the window, gazed out at the drabness of Berlin and listened to the tram noises and to the distant screeching of the U-Bahn as it took the big curve into the Zoo station. He gave a quick, reluctant glance at what he had examined the night before, noted that the weeds among the bomb rubble were much the same as the London ones – rose-bay willow-herb, dock and bracken – and then went into the kitchen. There was a note propped against a loaf of bread: 'My friend [a Secret Service euphemism which in this context meant Sender's chief] says it's all right for you to go out. But to be back by 1700 hours. Your gear [double-talk for Bond's rifle] has arrived and the batman will lay it out this pm. P. Sender.'

Bond lit the gas cooker, burned the message with a sneer at his profession, and then brewed himself a vast dish of scrambled eggs and bacon which he heaped on buttered toast and washed down with black coffee into which he had poured a liberal tot of whisky. Then he bathed and shaved, dressed in the drab, anonymous, middle-European clothes he had brought over for the purpose, looked at his disordered bed, decided to hell with it, and went down in the lift and out of the building.

James Bond had always found Berlin a glum, inimical city dry-varnished on the Western side with a brittle veneer of gimcrack polish, rather like the chromium trim on American motor-cars. He walked to the Kurfürsten-damm, sat in the Café Marquardt, drank an espresso and moodily watched the obedient queues of pedestrians waiting for the 'Go' sign on the traffic lights while the shiny stream of cars went through their dangerous quadrille at the busy intersection. It was cold outside and the sharp wind from the Russian steppes whipped at the girls' skirts and at the waterproofs of the impatient hurrying men each with the inevitable briefcase tucked under his arm. The infra-red wall heaters in the café glared redly down and gave a spurious glow to the faces of the café-squatters consuming their traditional 'one cup of coffee and ten glasses of water', reading the free newspapers and periodicals in their wooden racks or earnestly bent over business documents. Bond, closing his mind to the evening, debated with himself about ways to spend the afternoon. It finally came down to a choice between a visit to that respectable looking brownstone house in the Clausewitzstrasse, known to all concierges and taxi-drivers, or a trip to the Wannsee and a strenuous walk in the Grunewald. Virtue triumphed. Bond paid for his coffee, went out into the cold and took a taxi to the Zoo station.

The pretty young trees round the long lake had already been touched by the breath of autumn and there was occasional gold amongst the green. Bond walked hard for two hours along the leafy paths, then chose a restaurant with a glassed-in veranda above the lake and greatly enjoyed a high tea consisting of a double portion of matjes herrings smothered in cream and onion rings, and two 'Molle mit Korn', the Berlin equivalent of a 'boiler-maker and his assistant' – schnapps, doubles, washed down with draught Löwenbräu. Then, feeling more encouraged, he took the S-Bahn back into the city.

Outside the apartment house, a nondescript young man was tinkering with the engine of a black Opel Kapitan. He didn't take his head out from under the bonnet when Bond passed close by him and went up to the door and pressed the bell.

Captain Sender was reassuring. It was a 'friend' – a corporal from the transport section of Station WB. He had fixed up some bad engine trouble on the Opel. Each night, from six to seven, he would be ready to produce a series of multiple back-fires when a signal on a walkie-talkie operated by Sender told him to do so. This would give some kind of cover for the noise of Bond's shooting. Otherwise the neighbourhood might alert the police and there would be a lot of untidy explaining to be done. Their hideout was in the American sector and, while their American 'friends' had given Station WB clearance for this operation, the 'friends' were naturally anxious that it should be a clean job and without repercussions.

Bond was suitably impressed by the car gimmick, as he was by the very workmanlike preparations that had been made for him in the living-room. Here, behind the head of his high bed, giving a perfect firing position, a wood and metal stand had been erected against the broad window-sill and along it lay the Winchester, the tip of its barrel just denting the curtains. The wood and all the metal parts of the rifle and Sniperscope had been painted a dull black and, laid out on the bed like sinister evening clothes, was a black velvet hood stitched to a waist-length shirt of the same material. The hood had wide slits for the eyes and mouth. It reminded Bond of old prints of the Spanish Inquisition, or of the anonymous operators on the guillotine platform during the French Revolution. There was a similar hood on Captain Sender's bed, and on his section of the window-sill there lay a pair of night-glasses and the microphone for the walkie-talkie.

Captain Sender, his face worried and tense with nerves, said there was no news at the Station, no change in the situation as they knew it. Did Bond want anything to eat? Or a cup of tea? Perhaps a tranquillizer – there were several kinds in the bathroom?

Bond stitched a cheerful, relaxed expression on his face and said no thanks, and gave a light-hearted account of his day while an artery near his solar plexus began thumping gently as tension built up inside him like a watch-spring tightening. Finally his small talk petered out and he lay down on his bed with a German thriller he had bought on his wanderings, while Captain Sender moved fretfully about the flat, looking too often at his watch and chain-smoking Kent filter-tips through (he was a careful man) a Dunhill filter holder.

James Bond's choice of reading matter, prompted by a spectacular jacket of a half-naked girl strapped to a bed, turned out to have been a happy one for the occasion. It was called *Verderbt, Verdammt, Verraten*. The prefix *'ver'* signified that the girl had not only been ruined, damned and betrayed, but that she had suffered these misfortunes most thoroughly. James Bond temporarily lost himself in the tribulations of the heroine, Gräfin Liselotte Mutzenbacher, and it was with irritation that he heard Captain Sender say that it was five thirty and time to take up their positions.

Bond took off his coat and tie, put two sticks of chewing gum in his mouth and donned the hood. The lights were switched off by Captain Sender and Bond lay along the bed, got his eye to the eye-piece of the Sniperscope and gently lifted the bottom edge of the curtain back and over his shoulders.

Now dusk was approaching, but otherwise the scene, a year later to become famous as 'Checkpoint Charlie', was like a well-remembered photograph – the wasteland in front of him, the bright river of the frontier road, the farther waste-land and, on the left, the ugly square block of the Haus der Ministerien with its lit and dark windows. Bond scanned it all slowly, moving the Sniperscope, with the rifle, by means of the precision screws on the wooden base. It was all the same except that now there was a trickle of personnel leaving and entering the Ministry through the door on to the Wilhelmstrasse. Bond looked along at the four dark windows – dark again tonight – that he agreed with Sender were the enemy's firing points. The curtains were drawn back and the sash windows were wide open at the bottom. Bond's 'scope could not penetrate into the rooms, but there was no sign of movement within the four oblong, black, gaping mouths.

Now there was extra traffic in the street below. The women's orchestra came trooping down the pavement towards the entrance – twenty laughing, talking girls carrying their instruments – violin and wind instrument cases, satchels with their scores, and four of them with the drums – a gay, happy little crocodile. Bond was reflecting that some people still seemed to find life fun in the Soviet Sector, when his glasses picked out and stayed on the girl carrying the 'cello. Bond's masticating jaws stopped still and then reflectively went on with their chewing as he twisted the screw to depress the Sniperscope and keep her in its centre.

The girl was taller than the others and her long, straight, fair hair, falling to her shoulders, shone like molten gold under the arcs at the intersection. She was hurrying along in a charming, excited way, carrying the 'cello case as if it were no heavier than a violin. Everything was flying – the skirt of her coat, her feet, her hair. She was vivid with movement and life and, it seemed, with gaiety and happiness as she chattered to the two girls who flanked her and laughed back at what she was saying. As she turned in at the entrance amidst her troupe, the arcs momentarily caught a beautiful, pale profile. And then she was gone and, it seemed to Bond, with her disappearance a stab of grief lanced into his heart. How odd! How very odd! This had not happened to him since he was young. And now this single girl, seen only indistinctly and far away, had caused him to suffer this sharp pang of longing, this thrill of animal magnetism! Morosely, Bond glanced down at the luminous dial of his watch. Five fifty. Only ten minutes to go. No transport arriving at the entrance. None of those anonymous black Zik saloons he had half expected. He closed as much of his mind as he could to the girl and sharpened his wits. Get on, damn you! Get back to your job!

From somewhere inside the Ministry there came the familiar sounds of an orchestra tuning up – the strings tuning their instruments to single notes on the piano, the sharp blare of individual wood-winds – then a pause and then the collective crash of melody as the whole orchestra threw itself competently, so far as Bond could judge, into the opening bars of what even to James Bond was vaguely familiar.

'The Polovtsian Dances from *Prince Igor*,' said Captain Sender succinctly. 'Anyway, six o'clock coming up,' and then, urgently, 'Hey! Right-hand bottom of the four windows! Watch out!'

Bond minutely depressed the Sniperscope. Yes, there was movement inside the black cave. Now, from the interior, a thick black object, a weapon, had slid out. It moved firmly, minutely, swivelling down and sideways so as to cover the stretch of the Zimmerstrasse between the two waste-lands of rubble. Then the unseen operator in the room behind seemed satisfied and the weapon remained still, fixed obviously to a stand such as Bond had beneath his rifle.

'What is it? What sort of gun?' Captain Sender's voice was more breathless than it should have been. Take it easy, dammit! thought Bond. It's me who's supposed to have the nerves.

He strained his eyes, taking in the squat flash eliminator at the muzzle, the telescopic sight and thick downward chunk of magazine. Yes, that would be it! Absolutely for sure – and the best they had!

'Kalashnikov,' he said curtly. 'Sub-machine-gun. Gas operated. Thirty rounds in 7.62 millimetre. Favourite with the KGB. They're going to do a saturation job after all. Perfect for range. We'll have to get him pretty quick or 272'll end up not just dead but strawberry jam.

You keep an eye out for any movement over there in the rubble. I'll have to stay married to that window and the gun. He'll have to show himself to fire. Other chaps are probably spotting behind him – perhaps from all four windows. Much the sort of set-up we expected, but I didn't think they'd use a weapon that's going to make all the racket this one will. Should have known they would. A running man would be hard to get in this light with a single-shot job.'

Bond fiddled minutely with the traversing and elevating screws at his fingertips and got the fine lines of the 'scope exactly intersected, just behind where the butt of the enemy gun merged into the blackness behind. Get the chest – don't bother about the head!

Inside the hood, Bond's face began to sweat and his eye socket was slippery against the rubber of the eyepiece. That didn't matter. It was only his hands, his trigger-finger, that must stay bone dry. As the minutes ticked by, he frequently blinked his eyes to rest them, shifted his limbs to keep them supple, listened to the music to relax his mind.

The minutes slouched on leaden feet. How old would she be? Early twenties – say, twenty-three. With that poise and insouciance, the hint of authority in her long easy stride, she would come of good racy stock – one of the old Prussian families probably, or from similar remnants in Poland or even Russia. Why in hell did she have to choose the 'cello? There was something almost indecent in the idea of that bulbous, ungainly instrument between her splayed thighs. Of course Suggia had managed to look elegant, and so did that girl Amaryllis somebody. But they should invent a way for women to play the damned thing side-saddle.

At his side Captain Sender said, 'Seven o'clock. Nothing's stirred on the other side. Bit of movement on our side, near a cellar close to the frontier; that'll be our reception committee – two good men from the Station. Better stay with it until they close down. Let me know when they take that gun in.'

'All right.'

It was seven thirty when the KGB sub-machine-gun was gently drawn back into the black interior. One by one the bottom sashes of the four windows were closed. The cold-hearted game was over for the night. 272 was still holed up. Two more nights to go!

Bond softly drew the curtain over his shoulders and across the muzzle of the Winchester. He got up, pulled off his cowl and went into the bathroom and stripped and had a shower. Then he had two large whiskies on the rocks in quick succession, while he waited, his ears pricked, for the now muffled sound of the orchestra to stop. When at eight o'clock it did (with the expert

27

comment from Sender, 'Borodin's *Prince Igor*, Choral Dance Number 17, I think,') he said to Sender, who had been getting off his report in garbled language to the Head of Station, 'Just going to have another look. I've rather taken to that tall blonde with the 'cello.'

'Didn't notice her,' said Sender, uninterested. He went into the kitchen. Tea, guessed Bond. Or perhaps Horlicks. Bond donned his cowl, went back to his firing position and depressed the Sniperscope to the doorway of the Ministry. Yes, there they went, not so gay and laughing now. Tired, perhaps. And now here she came, less lively but still with that beautiful careless stride. Bond watched the blown, golden hair and the fawn raincoat until it had vanished into the indigo dusk up the Wilhelmstrasse. Where did she live? In some miserable, flaked room in the suburbs? Or in one of the privileged apartments in the hideous, lavatory-tiled Stalinallee?

Bond drew himself back. Somewhere, within easy reach, that girl lived. Was she married? Did she have a lover? Anyway to hell with it! She was not for him.

The next day, and the next night-watch, were duplicates, with small variations, of the first. James Bond had two more brief rendezvous, by Sniperscope, with the girl, and the rest was a killing of time and a tightening of the tension that, by the time the third and final day came, was like a fog in the small room.

James Bond crammed the third day with an almost lunatic programme of museums, art galleries, the zoo and a film, hardly perceiving anything he looked at, his mind's eye divided between the girl and those four black squares and the black tube and the unknown man behind it – the man he was now certainly going to kill tonight.

Back in the apartment punctually at five, Bond narrowly averted a row with Captain Sender, because he had poured himself a stiff whisky before putting on the hideous cowl that now stank of his sweat. Captain Sender had tried to prevent him and, when he failed, had threatened to call up Head of Station and report Bond for breaking training.

'Look, my friend,' said Bond wearily, 'I've got to commit a murder tonight. Not you. Me. So be a good chap and stuff it, would you? You can tell Tanqueray anything you like when it's over. Think I like this job? Having a Double-O number and so on? I'd be quite happy for you to get me sacked from the Double-O Section. Then I could settle down and make a snug nest of papers as an ordinary Staffer. Right?' Bond drank down his whisky, reached for his thriller, now arriving at an appalling climax, and threw himself on the bed.

Captain Sender, icily silent, went off into the kitchen to brew, from the sounds, his inevitable cuppa.

Bond felt the whisky beginning to melt the coiled nerves in his stomach. Now then, Liselotte, how in hell are you going to get out of this fix?

It was exactly six five when Sender, at his post, began talking excitedly. 'Bond, there's something moving way back over there. Now he's stopped – wait, no, he's on the move again, keeping low. There's a bit of broken wall there. He'll be out of sight of the opposition. But thick weeds, yards of them, ahead of him. Christ! He's coming through the weeds. And they're moving. Hope to God they think it's only the wind.

' 'Now he's through and gone to ground. Any reaction?'

'No,' said Bond tensely. 'Keep on telling me. How far to the frontier?'

'He's only got about fifty yards to go.' Captain Sender's voice was harsh with excitement. 'Broken stuff, but some of it's open. Then a solid chunk of wall right up against the pavement. He'll have to get over it. They can't fail to spot him then. Now! Now he's made ten yards, and another ten. Got him clearly then. Blackened his face and hands. Get ready! Any moment now he'll make the last sprint.'

James Bond felt the sweat pouring down his face and neck. He took a chance and quickly wiped his hands down his sides and then got them back to the rifle, his finger inside the guard, just lying along the curved trigger. 'There's something moving in the room behind the gun. They must have spotted him. Get that Opel working.'

Bond heard the code word go into the microphone, heard the Opel in the street below start up, felt his pulse quicken as the engine leaped into life and a series of ear-splitting cracks came from the exhaust.

The movement in the black cave was now definite. A black arm with a black glove had reached out and under the stock.

'Now!' ejaculated Captain Sender. 'Now! He's run for the wall! He's up it! Just going to jump!'

And then, in the Sniperscope, Bond saw the head of 'Trigger' – the purity of the profile, the golden bell of hair – all laid out along the stock of the Kalashnikov! She was dead, a sitting duck! Bond's fingers flashed down to the screws, inched them round and, as yellow flame fluttered at the snout of the sub-machine-gun, squeezed the trigger.

The bullet, dead on at three hundred and ten yards, must have hit where the stock ended up the barrel, might have got her in the left hand, but the effect was to tear the gun off its mountings, smash it against the side of the window-frame and then hurl it out of the window. It turned several times on its way down and crashed into the middle of the street.

'He's over!' shouted Captain Sender. 'He's over! He's done it! My God, he's done it!'

'Get down! said Bond sharply, and threw himself sideways off the bed as the big eye of a searchlight in one of the black windows blazed on, swerving up the street towards their block and their room. Then gunfire crashed and the bullets howled into their window, ripping the curtains, smashing the woodwork, thudding into the walls.

Behind the roar and zing of the bullets, Bond heard the Opel race off down the street and, behind that again, the fragmentary whisper of the orchestra. The combination of the two background noises clicked. Of course! The orchestra had probably raised an infernal din throughout the Haus der Ministerien, having been used, like the backfiring Opel on this side, to provide some cover for a sharp burst of fire, on their side by 'Trigger'. Had she carried her weapon to and fro every day in that 'cello case? Was the whole orchestra composed of KGB women? Had the other instrument cases contained only equipment – the big drum perhaps the searchlight – while the real instruments were available in the concert hall? Too elaborate? Too fantastic? Probably. But there had been no doubt about the girl. In the Sniperscope, Bond had even been able to see one wide, heavily lashed, aiming eye. Had he hurt her? Almost certainly her left arm. There would be no chance of seeing her, seeing how she was, if she left with the orchestra. Now he would never see her again. Their window would be a death trap. To underline the fact, a stray bullet smashed into the mechanism of the Winchester, already overturned and damaged, and hot lead splashed down on Bond's hand, burning the skin. On Bond's emphatic oath, abruptly the firing stopped and silence sang in the room.

Captain Sender emerged from beside his bed, brushing glass out of his hair. They crunched across the floor and through the splintered door into the kitchen. Here, because it faced away from the street, it was safe to switch on the light.

'Any damage?' asked Bond.

'No. You all right?' Captain Sender's pale eyes were bright with the fever that comes in battle. They also, Bond noticed, held a sharp glint of accusation.

'Yes. Just get an Elastoplast for my hand. Caught a splash from one of the bullets.' Bond went into the bathroom. When he came out, Captain Sender was sitting by the walkie-talkie he had fetched from the sitting-room. He was speaking into it. Now he said into the microphone, 'That's all for now. Fine about 272. Hurry the armoured car, if you would. Be glad to get out of here, and 007 will need to write his version of what happened. Okay? Then OVER and OUT.'

Captain Sender turned to Bond. Half accusing, half embarrassed, he said, 'Afraid Head of Station needs your reasons in writing for not getting that chap. I had to tell him I'd seen you alter your aim at the last second. Gave "Trigger" time to get off a burst. Damned lucky for 272 he'd just begun his sprint. Blew chunks off the wall behind him. What was it all about?'

James Bond knew he could lie, knew he could fake a dozen reasons why. Instead he took a deep pull at the strong whisky he had poured for himself, put the glass down and looked Captain Sender straight in the eye.

'"Trigger" was a woman.'

'So what? KGB have got plenty of women agents – and women gunners. I'm not in the least surprised. The Russian women's team always does well in the World Championships. Last meeting, in Moscow, they came first, second and third against seven countries. I can even remember two of their names – Donskaya and Lomova, terrific shots. She may even have been one of them. What did she look like? Records'll probably be able to turn her up.'

'She was a blonde. She was the girl who carried the 'cello in that orchestra. Probably had her gun in the 'cello case. The orchestra was to cover up the shooting.'

'Oh!' said Captain Sender slowly, 'I see. The girl you were keen on?'

'That's right.'

'Well, I'm sorry, but I'll have to put that in my report too. You had clear orders to exterminate "Trigger".'

There came the sound of a car approaching. It pulled up somewhere below. The bell rang twice. Sender said, 'Well, let's get going. They've sent an armoured car to get us out of here.' He paused. His eyes flicked over Bond's shoulder, avoiding Bond's eyes. 'Sorry about the report. Got to do my duty, y'know. You should have killed that sniper whoever it was.'

Bond got up. He suddenly didn't want to leave the stinking little smashed-up flat, leave the place from which, for three days, he had had this long-range, one-sided romance with an unknown girl – an unknown enemy agent with much the same job in her outfit as he had in his. Poor little bitch! She would be in worse trouble now than he was! She'd certainly be court-martialled for muffing this job. Probably be kicked out of the KGB. He shrugged. At least they'd stop short of killing her – as he himself had done.

James Bond said wearily, 'Okay. With any luck it'll

cost me my Double-O number. But tell Head of Station not to worry. That girl won't do any more sniping. Probably lost her left hand. Certainly broke her nerve for that kind of work. Scared the living daylights out of her. In my book, that was enough. Let's go.'

From a View to a Kill

The eyes behind the wide black rubber goggles were cold as flint. In the howling speed-turmoil of a BSA M20 doing seventy, they were the only quiet things in the hurtling flesh and metal. Protected by the glass of the goggles, they stared fixedly ahead from just above the centre of the handlebars, and their dark unwavering focus was that of gun muzzles. Below the goggles, the wind had got into the face through the mouth and had wrenched the lips back into a square grin that showed big tombstone teeth and strips of whitish gum. On both sides of the grin the cheeks had been blown out by the wind into pouches that fluttered slightly. To right and left of the hurtling face under the crash helmet, the black gauntlets, broken-wristed at the controls, looked like the attacking paws of a big animal.

The man was dressed in the uniform of a dispatch-rider in the Royal Corps of Signals, and his machine, painted olive green, was, with certain modifications to the valves and the carburettor and the removal of some of the silencer baffles to give more speed, identical with a standard British Army machine. There was nothing in the man or his equipment to suggest that he was not what he appeared to be, except a fully loaded Luger held by a clip to the top of the petrol tank.

It was seven o'clock on a May morning and the dead straight road through the forest glittered with the tiny luminous mist of spring. On both sides of the road the moss- and flower-carpeted depths between the great oak trees held the theatrical enchantment of the royal forests of Versailles and St Germain. The road was D98, a secondary road serving local traffic in the St Germain area, and the motor-cyclist had just passed beneath the Paris-Mantes autoroute already thundering with commuter traffic for Paris. He was heading north towards St Germain and there was no one else in sight in either direction, except, perhaps half a mile ahead, an almost identical figure – another Royal Corps dispatch-rider. He was a younger, slimmer man and he sat comfortably back on his machine, enjoying the morning and keeping his speed to around forty. He was well on time and it was a beautiful day. He wondered whether to have his eggs fried or scrambled when he got back to HQ around eight.

Five hundred yards, four hundred, three, two, one.

The man coming up from behind slowed to fifty. He put his right gauntlet up to his teeth and pulled it off. He stuffed the gauntlet between the buttons of his tunic and reached down and unclipped the gun.

By now he must have been big in the driving-mirror of the young man ahead, for suddenly the young man jerked his head round, surprised to find another dispatch-rider on his run at that time of the morning. He expected that it would be an American or perhaps French military police. It might be anyone from the eight NATO nations that made up the staff of SHAPE, but when he recognized the uniform of the Corps he was astonished and delighted. Who the hell could it be? He raised a cheerful right thumb in recognition and cut his speed to thirty, waiting for the other man to drift up alongside. With one eye on the road ahead and the other on the approaching silhouette in the mirror, he ran through the names of the British riders in the Special Service Transportation Unit at Headquarters Command. Albert, Sid, Wally – might be Wally, same thick build. Good show! He'd be able to pull his leg about that little frog bit in the canteen – Louise, Elise, Lise – what the hell was her name.

The man with the gun had slowed. Now he was fifty yards away. His face, undistorted by the wind, had set into blunt, hard, perhaps Slav lines. A red spark burned behind the black, aimed muzzles of the eyes. Forty yards, thirty. A single magpie flew out of the forest ahead of the young dispatch-rider. It fled clumsily across the road into the bushes behind a Michelin sign that said that St Germain was one kilometre to go. The young man grinned and raised an ironical finger in salute and self-protection – 'One magpie is sorrow'.

Twenty yards behind him the man with the gun took both hands off the handlebars, lifted the Luger, rested it carefully on his left forearm and fired one shot.

The young man's hands whipped off his controls and met across the centre of his backward-arching spine. His machine veered across the road, jumped a narrow ditch and ploughed into a patch of grass and lilies of the valley. There it rose up on its screaming back wheel and slowly crashed backwards on top of its dead rider. The BSA coughed and kicked and tore at the young man's clothes and at the flowers, and then lay quiet.

The killer executed a narrow turn and stopped with his machine pointing back the way he had come. He stamped down the wheel-rest, pulled his machine up on to it and walked in among the wild flowers under the trees. He knelt down beside the dead man and brusquely pulled back an eyelid. Just as roughly he tore the black leather dispatch-case off the corpse and ripped open the buttons of the tunic and removed a battered leather wallet. He wrenched a cheap wristwatch so sharply off the left wrist that the chrome expanding bracelet snapped in half. He stood up and slung the dispatch-case over his shoulder. While he stowed the wallet and the watch away in his tunic pocket he listened. There were only forest sounds and the slow tick of hot metal from the crashed BSA. The killer retraced his steps to the road. He walked slowly, scuffing leaves over the tyre marks in the soft earth and moss. He took extra trouble over the deep scars in the ditch and the grass verge, and then stood beside his motor-cycle and looked back towards the lily of the valley patch. Not bad! Probably only the police dogs would get it, and, with ten miles of road to cover, they would be hours, perhaps days – plenty long enough. The main thing in these jobs was to have enough safety margin. He could have shot the man at forty yards, but he had preferred to get to twenty. And taking the watch and the wallet had been nice touches – pro touches.

Pleased with himself, the man heaved his machine off its rest, vaulted smartly into the saddle and kicked down on the starter. Slowly, so as not to show skid marks, he accelerated away back down the road and in a minute or so he was doing seventy again and the wind had redrawn the empty turnip grin across his face.

Around the scene of the killing, the forest, which

had held its breath while it was done, slowly began to breathe again.

James Bond had his first drink of the evening at Fouquet's. It was not a solid drink. One cannot drink seriously in French cafés. Out of doors on a pavement in the sun is no place for vodka or whisky or gin. A *fine à l'eau* is fairly serious, but it intoxicates without tasting very good. A *quart de champagne* or a *champagne à l'orange* is all right before luncheon, but in the evening one *quart* leads to another *quart* and a bottle of indifferent champagne is a bad foundation for the night. Pernod is possible, but it should be drunk in company, and anyway Bond had never liked the stuff because its liquorice taste reminded him of his childhood. No, in cafés you have to drink the least offensive of the musical comedy drinks that go with them, and Bond always had the same thing – an Americano – Bitter Campari, Cinzano, a large slice of lemon peel and soda. For the soda he always stipulated Perrier, for in his opinion expensive soda water was the cheapest way to improve a poor drink.

When Bond was in Paris he invariably stuck to the same addresses. He stayed at the Terminus Nord, because he liked station hotels and because this was the least pretentious and most anonymous of them. He had luncheon at the Café de la Paix, the Rotonde or the Dôme, because the food was good enough and it amused him to watch the people. If he wanted a solid drink he had it at Harry's Bar, both because of the solidity of the drinks and because, on his first ignorant visit to Paris at the age of sixteen, he had done what Harry's advertisement in the *Continental Daily Mail* had told him to do and had said to his taxi-driver 'Sank Roo Doe Noo'. That had started one of the memorable evenings of his life, culminating in the loss, almost simultaneous, of his virginity and his note-case. For dinner, Bond went to one of the great restaurants – Véfour, the Caneton, Lucas-Carton or the Cochon d'Or. These he considered, whatever Michelin might say about the Tour d'Argent, Maxims and the like, to have somehow avoided the tarnish of the expense account and the dollar. Anyway, he preferred their cooking. After dinner he generally went to the Place Pigalle to see what would happen to him. When, as usual, nothing did, he would walk home across Paris to the Gare du Nord and go to bed.

Tonight Bond decided to tear up this dusty address-book and have himself an old-fashioned ball. He was on his way through Paris after a dismally failed assignment on the Austro-Hungarian border. It had been a question of getting a certain Hungarian out. Bond had been sent from London specially to direct the operation over the head of Station V. This had been unpopular with the Vienna Station. There had been misunderstandings – wilful ones. The man had been killed in the frontier minefield. There would have to be a court of inquiry. Bond was due back at his London headquarters on the following day to make his report, and the thought of it all depressed him. Today had been so beautiful – one of those days when you almost believe that Paris is beautiful and gay – and Bond had decided to give the town just one more chance. He would somehow find himself a girl who was a real girl, and he would take her to dinner at some make-believe place in the Bois like the Armenonville. To clean the money-look out of her eyes – for it would certainly be there – he would as soon as possible give her fifty thousand francs. He would say to her: 'I propose to call you Donatienne, or possibly Solange, because these are names that suit my mood and the evening. We knew each other before and you lent me this money because I was in a jam. Here it is, and now we will tell each other what we have been doing since we last met in St Tropez just a year ago. In the meantime, here is the menu and the wine list and you must choose what will make you happy and fat.' And she would look relieved at not having to try any more, and she would laugh and say: 'But, James, I do not want to be fat.' And there they would be, started on the myth of 'Paris in the Spring', and Bond would stay sober and be interested in her and everything she said. And, by God, by the end of the evening it would not be his fault if it transpired that there was in fact no shred of stuffing left in the hoary old fairytale of 'A good time in Paris'.

Sitting in Fouquet's, waiting for his Americano, Bond smiled at his vehemence. He knew that he was only playing at this fantasy for the satisfaction of launching a last kick at a town he had cordially disliked since the War. Since 1945, he had not had a happy day in Paris. It was not that the town had sold its body. Many towns have done that. It was its heart that was gone – pawned to the tourists, pawned to the Russians and Roumanians and Bulgars, pawned to the scum of the world who had gradually taken the town over. And, of course, pawned to the Germans. You could see it in the people's eyes – sullen, envious, ashamed. Architecture? Bond glanced across the pavement at the shiny black ribbons of cars off which the sun glinted painfully. Everywhere it was the same as in the Champs-Elysées. There were only two hours in which you could even see the town – between five and seven in the morning. After seven it was engulfed in a thundering stream of black metal with which no beautiful buildings, no spacious, tree-lined boulevards, could compete.

The waiter's tray clattered down on the marble-topped table. With a slick one-handed jerk that Bond had never been able to copy, the waiter's bottle-opener prised the cap off the Perrier. The man slipped the tab under the ice-bucket, said a mechanical 'Voilà, M'sieur' and darted away. Bond put ice into his drink, filled it to the top with soda and took a long pull at it. He sat back and lit a Laurens jaune. Of course the evening would be a disaster. Even supposing he found the girl in the next hour or so, the contents would certainly not stand up to the wrapping. On closer examination she would turn out to have the heavy, dank, wide-pored skin of the bourgeois French. The blonde hair under the rakish velvet beret would be brown at the roots and as coarse as piano wire. The peppermint on the breath would not conceal the midday garlic. The alluring figure would be intricately scaffolded with wire and rubber. She would be from Lille and she would ask him if he was American. And, Bond smiled to himself, she or her *maquereau* would probably steal his note-case. La ronde! He would be back where he came in. More or less, that was. Well, to hell with it!

A battered black Peugeot 403 broke out of the centre stream of traffic, cut across the inside line of cars and pulled in to double park at the kerb. There was the usual screaming of brakes, hooting and yelling. Quite unmoved, a girl got out of the car and, leaving the traffic to sort itself out, walked purposefully across the sidewalk. Bond sat up. She had everything, but absolutely everything that belonged in his fantasy. She was tall and, although her figure was hidden by a light raincoat, the way she moved and the way she held herself promised that it would be beautiful. The face had the gaiety and bravado that went with her driving, but now there was impatience in the compressed lips and the eyes fretted as she pushed diagonally through the moving crowd on the pavement.

Bond watched her narrowly as she reached the edge of the tables and came up the aisle. Of course it was hopeless. She was coming to meet someone – her lover. She was the sort of woman who always belongs to somebody else. She was late for him. That's why she was in such a hurry. What damnable luck – right down to the long blonde hair under the rakish beret! And she was looking straight at him. She was smiling . . . !

Before Bond could pull himself together, the girl had come up to his table and had drawn out a chair and sat down.

She smiled rather tautly into his startled eyes. 'I'm sorry I'm late, and I'm afraid we've got to get moving at once. You're wanted at the office.' She added under her breath: 'Crash dive.'

Bond jerked himself back to reality. Whoever she was, she was certainly from 'the firm'. 'Crash dive' was a slang expression the Secret Service had borrowed from the Submarine Service. It meant bad news – the worst. Bond dug into his pocket and slid some coins over the table. He said 'Right. Let's go,' and got up and followed her down through the tables and across to her car. It was still obstructing the inner lane of traffic. Any minute now there would be a policeman. Angry faces glared at them as they climbed in. The girl had left the engine running. She banged the gears into second and slid out into the traffic.

Bond looked sideways at her. The pale skin was velvet. The blonde hair was silk – to the roots. He said: 'Where are you from and what's it all about?'

She said, concentrating on the traffic: 'From the Station. Grade two assistant. Number 765 on duty, Mary Ann Russell off. I've no idea what it's all about. I just saw the signal from HQ – personal from M to Head of Station. Most Immediate and all that. He was to find you at once and if necessary use the Deuxième to help. Head of F said you always went to the same places when you were in Paris, and I and another girl were given a list.' She smiled. 'I'd only tried Harry's Bar, and after Fouquet's I was going to start on the restaurants. It was marvellous picking you up like that.' She gave him a quick glance. 'I hope I wasn't very clumsy.'

Bond said: 'You were fine. How were you going to handle it if I'd had a girl with me?'

She laughed. 'I was going to do much the same except call you "sir". I was only worried about how you'd dispose of the girl. If she started a scene I was going to offer to take her home in my car and for you to take a taxi.'

'You sound pretty resourceful. How long have you been in the Service?'

'Five years. This is my first time with a Station.'

'How do you like it?'

'I like the work all right. The evenings and days off drag a bit. It's not easy to make friends in Paris without' – her mouth turned down with irony – 'without all the rest. I mean,' she hastened to add, 'I'm not a prude and all that, but somehow the French make the whole business such a bore. I mean I've had to give up taking the Metro or buses. Whatever time of day it is, you end up with your behind black and blue.' She laughed. 'Apart from the boredom of it and not knowing what to say to the man, some of the pinches really hurt. It's the limit. So to get around I bought this car cheap, and other cars seem to keep out of my way. As long as you don't catch the other driver's eye, you can take on even the meanest of them. They're afraid you haven't seen them. And they're worried by the bashed-about look of the car. They give you a wide berth.'

They had come to the Rond Point. As if to demonstrate her theory, she tore round it and went straight at the line of traffic coming up from the Place de la Concorde. Miraculously it divided and let her through into the Avenue Matignon.

Bond said: 'Pretty good. But don't make it a habit. There may be some French Mary Anns about.'

She laughed. She turned into the Avenue Gabrielle and pulled up outside the Paris headquarters of the Secret Service: 'I only try that sort of manœuvre in the line of duty.'

Bond got out and came round to her side of the car. He said: 'Well, thanks for picking me up. When this whirl is over, can I pick you up in exchange? I don't get the pinches, but I'm just as bored in Paris as you are.'

Her eyes were blue and wide apart. They searched his. She said seriously: 'I'd like that. The switchboard here can always find me.'

Bond reached in through the window and pressed the hand on the wheel. He said 'Good,' and turned and walked quickly in through the archway.

Wing Commander Rattray, Head of Station F, was a fattish man with pink cheeks and fair hair brushed straight back. He dressed in a mannered fashion with turned-back cuffs and double slits to his coat, bow-ties and fancy waistcoats. He made a good-living, wine-and-food-society impression in which only the slow, rather cunning blue eyes struck a false note. He chain-smoked Gauloises and his office stank of them. He greeted Bond with relief. 'Who found you?'

'Russell. At Fouquet's. Is she new?'

'Six months. She's a good one. But take a pew. There's the hell of a flap on and I've got to brief you and get you going.' He bent to his intercom and pressed down a switch. 'Signal to M, please. Personal from Head of Station. "Located 007 briefing now." Okay?' He let go the switch.

Bond pulled a chair over by the open window to keep away from the fog of Gauloises. The traffic on the Champs-Elysées was a soft roar in the background. Half an hour before he had been fed up with Paris, glad to be going. Now he hoped he would be staying.

Head of F said: 'Somebody got our dawn dispatch-rider from SHAPE to the St Germain Station yesterday morning. The weekly run from the SHAPE Intelligence Division with the Summaries, Joint Intelligence papers, Iron Curtain Order of Battle – all the top gen. One shot in the back. Took his dispatch-case and his wallet and watch.'

Bond said: 'That's bad. No chance that it was an ordinary hold-up? Or do they think the wallet and watch were cover?'

'SHAPE Security can't make up their minds. On the whole they guess it was cover. Seven o'clock in the morning's a rum time for a hold-up. But you can argue it out with them when you get down there. M's sending you as his personal representative. He's worried as hell. Apart from the loss of the Intelligence dope, their I. people have never liked having one of our Stations outside the Reservation so to speak. For years they've been trying to get the St Germain unit incorporated in the SHAPE Intelligence set-up. But you know what M is, independent old devil. He's never been happy about NATO Security. Why, right in the SHAPE Intelligence Division there are not only a couple of Frenchmen and an Italian, but the head of their Counter Intelligence and Security section is a German!'

Bond whistled.

'The trouble is that this damnable business is all SHAPE needs to bring M to heel. Anyway, he says you're to get down there right away. I've fixed up clearance for you. Got the passes. You're to report to Colonel Schreiber, Headquarters Command Security Branch. American. Efficient chap. He's been handling the thing from the beginning. As far as I can gather, he's already done just about all there was to be done.'

'What's he done? What actually happened?'

Head of F picked up a map from his desk and walked over with it. It was the big-scale Michelin *Environs de Paris*. He pointed with a pencil. 'Here's Versailles, and here, just north of the park, is the big junction of the Paris-Mantes and the Versailles autoroutes. A couple of hundred yards north of that, on N184, is SHAPE. Every Wednesday, at seven in the morning, a Special Services dispatch-rider leaves SHAPE with the weekly Intelligence stuff I told you about. He has to get to this little village called Fourqueux, just outside St Germain, deliver his stuff to the duty officer at our HQ, and report back to SHAPE by seven-thirty. Rather than go through all this builtup area, for security reasons his orders are to take this N307 to St Nom, turn right-handed on to D98 and go under the autoroute and through the forest of St Germain. The distance is about twelve kilometres, and taking it easy he'll do the trip in under a quarter of an hour. Well, yesterday it was a corporal from the Corps of Signals, good solid man called Bates, and when he hadn't reported back to SHAPE by seven-forty-five they sent another rider to look for him. Not a trace, and he hadn't reported at our HQ. By eight-fifteen the Security Branch was on the job, and by nine the road-blocks were up. The police and the Deuxième were told and search parties got under way. The dogs found him, but not till the evening around six, and by that time if there had been any clues on the road they'd have been wiped out by the traffic.' Head of F handed the map to Bond and walked back to his desk. 'And that's about the lot, except that all the usual steps have been taken – frontiers, ports, aerodromes and so forth. But that sort of thing won't help. If it was a professional job, who- ever did it could have had the stuff out of the country by midday or into an embassy in Paris inside an hour.'

Bond said impatiently: 'Exactly! And so what the hell does M expect me to do? Tell SHAPE Security to do it all over again, but better? This sort of thing isn't my line at all. Bloody waste of time.'

Head of F smiled sympathetically. 'Matter of fact I put much the same point of view to M over the scram- bler. Tactfully. The old man was quite reasonable. Said he wanted to show SHAPE he was taking the business just as seriously as they were. You happened to be avail- able and more or less on the spot, and he said you had the sort of mind that might pick up the invisible factor. I asked him what he meant, and he said that at all closely guarded headquarters there's bound to be an invisible man – a man everyone takes so much for granted that he just isn't noticed – gardener, window cleaner, post- man. I said that SHAPE had thought of that, and that all those sort of jobs were done by enlisted men. M told me not to be so literal-minded and hung up.'

Bond laughed. He could see M's frown and hear the crusty voice. He said: 'All right, then. I'll see what I can do. Who do I report back to?'

'Here. M doesn't want the St Germain unit to get involved. Anything you have to say I'll put straight on the printer to London. But I may not be available when you call up. I'll make someone your duty officer and you'll be able to get them any time in the twenty-four hours. Russell can do it. She picked you up. She might as well carry you. Suit you?'

'Yes,' said Bond. 'That'll be all right.'

The battered Peugeot, commandeered by Rattray, smelled of her. There were bits of her in the glove compartment – half a packet of Suchard milk chocolate, a twist of paper containing bobby pins, a paperback John O'Hara, a single black suede glove. Bond thought about her as far as the Etoile and then closed his mind to her and pushed the car along fast through the Bois. Rattray had said it would take about fifteen minutes at fifty. Bond said to halve the speed and double the time and to tell Colonel Schreiber that he would be with him by nine-thirty. After the Porte de St Cloud there was little traffic, and Bond held seventy on the autoroute until the second exit road came up on his right and there was the red arrow for SHAPE. Bond turned up the slope and on to N184. Two hundred yards farther, in the centre of the road, was the traffic policeman Bond had been told to look out for. The policeman waved him in through the big gates on the left and he pulled up at the first checkpoint. A grey-uniformed American policeman hung out of his cabin and glanced at his pass. He was told to pull inside and hold it. Now a French policeman took his pass, noted the details on a printed form clipped to a board, gave him a large plastic wind-screen number and waved him on. As Bond pulled in to the car park, with theatrical suddenness a hundred arc-lights blazed and lit up the acre of low-lying hut-ments in front of him as if it was day. Feeling naked, Bond walked across the open gravel beneath the flags of the NATO countries and ran up the four shallow steps to the wide glass doors that gave entrance to the Supreme Headquarters Allied Forces Europe. Now there was the main Security desk. American and French military police checked his pass and noted the details. He was handed over to a red-capped British MP and led off down the main corridor past endless office doors. They bore no names but the usual alphabetical abraca-dabra of all headquarters. One said COMSTRIKFLTLANT AND SACLANT LIAISON TO SACEUR. Bond asked what it meant. The military policeman, either ignorant or, more probably, security-minded, said stolidly: 'Couldn't rightly say, sir.'

Behind a door that said *Colonel G. A. Schreiber, Chief of Security, Headquarters Command*, was a ramrod-straight, middle-aged American with greying hair and the politely negative manner of a bank manager. There were several family photographs in silver frames on his desk and a vase containing one white rose. There was no smell of tobacco smoke in the room. After cautiously amiable preliminaries, Bond congratulated the Colonel on his security. He said: 'All these checks and double checks don't make it easy for the opposition. Have you ever lost anything before, or have you ever found signs of a serious attempt at a coup?'

'No to both questions, Commander. I'm quite satisfied about Headquarters. It's only the outlying units that worry me. Apart from this section of your Secret Service, we have various detached signal units. Then, of course, there are the Home Ministries of fourteen different nations. I can't answer for what may leak from those quarters.'

'It can't be an easy job,' agreed Bond. 'Now, about this mess. Has anything else come up since Wing Commander Rattray spoke to you last?'

'Got the bullet. Luger. Severed the spinal cord. Probably fired at around thirty yards, give or take ten yards.

Assuming our man was riding a straight course, the bullet must have been fired from dead astern on a level trajectory. Since it can't have been a man standing in the road, the killer must have been moving in or on some vehicle.'

'So your man would have seen him in the driving-mirror?'

'Probably.'

'If your riders find themselves being followed, do they have any instructions about taking evasive action?'

The Colonel smiled slightly. 'Sure. They're told to go like hell.'

'And at what speed did your man crash?'

'Not fast, they think. Between twenty and forty. What are you getting at, Commander?'

'I was wondering if you'd decided whether it was a pro or an amateur job. If your man wasn't trying to get away, and assuming he saw the killer in his mirror, which I agree is only a probability, that suggests that he accepted the man on his tail as friend rather than foe. That could mean some sort of disguise that would fit in with the set-up here – something your man would accept even at that hour of the morning.'

A small frown had been gathering across Colonel Schreiber's smooth forehead. 'Commander,' there was an edge of tension in the voice, 'we have, of course, been considering every angle of this case, including the one you mention. At midday yesterday the Commanding General declared emergency in this matter, standing security and security ops committees were set up, and from that moment on every angle, every hint of a clue, has been systematically run to earth. And I can tell you, Commander,' the Colonel raised one well-manicured hand and let it descend in soft emphasis on his blotting-pad, 'any man who can come up with an even remotely original idea on this case will have to be closely related to Einstein. There is nothing, repeat nothing, to go on in this case whatsoever.'

Bond smiled sympathetically. He got to his feet. 'In that case, Colonel, I won't waste any more of your time this evening. If I could just have the minutes of the various meetings to bring myself up to date, and if one of your men could show me the way to the canteen and my quarters . . .'

'Sure, sure.' The Colonel pressed a bell. A young crew-cutted aide came in. 'Proctor, show the Commander to his room in the VIP wing, would you, and then take him along to the bar and the canteen.' He turned to Bond. 'I'll have those papers ready for you after you've had a meal and a drink. They'll be in my office. They can't be taken out, of course, but you'll find everything to hand next door, and Proctor will be able to fill you in on anything that's missing.' He held out his hand. 'Okay? Then we'll meet again in the morning.'

Bond said goodnight and followed the aide out. As he walked along the neutral-painted, neutral-smelling corridors, he reflected that this was probably the most hopeless assignment he had ever been on. If the top security brains of fourteen countries were stumped, what hope had he got? By the time he was in bed that night, in the Spartan luxury of the visitors' overnight quarters, Bond had decided he would give it a couple more days – largely for the sake of keeping in touch with Mary Ann Russell for as long as possible – and then chuck it. On this decision he fell immediately into a deep and untroubled sleep.

Not two, but four days later, as the dawn came up over the Forest of St Germain, James Bond was lying along the thick branch of an oak tree keeping watch over a small empty glade that lay deep among the trees bordering D98, the road of the murder.

He was dressed from head to foot in parachutists' camouflage – green, brown and black. Even his hands were covered with the stuff, and there was a hood over his head with slits cut for the eyes and mouth. It was good camouflage which would be still better when the sun was higher and the shadows blacker, and from anywhere on the ground, even directly below the high branch, he could not be seen.

It had come about like this. The first two days at SHAPE had been the expected waste of time. Bond had achieved nothing except to make himself mildly unpopular with the persistence of his double-checking questions. On the morning of the third day he was about to go and say his goodbyes when he had a telephone call from the Colonel. 'Oh, Commander, thought I'd let you know that the last team of police dogs got in late last night – your idea that it might be worth while covering the whole forest. Sorry' – the voice sounded un-sorry – 'but negative, absolutely negative.'

'Oh. My fault for the wasted time.' As much to annoy the Colonel as anything, Bond said: 'Mind if I have a talk with the handler?'

'Sure, sure. Anything you want. By the way, Commander, how long are you planning to be around? Glad to have you with us for as long as you like. But it's a question of your room. Seems there's a big party coming in from Holland in a few days' time. Top level staff course or something of the kind, and Admin says they're a bit pushed for space.'

Bond had not expected to get on well with Colonel Schreiber and he had not done so. He said amiably:

'I'll see what my Chief has to say and call you back, Colonel.'

'Do that, would you.' The Colonel's voice was equally polite, but the manners of both men were running out and the two receivers broke the line simultaneously.

The chief handler was a Frenchman from the Landes. He had the quick sly eyes of a poacher. Bond met him at the kennels, but the handler's proximity was too much for the Alsatians and, to get away from the noise, he took Bond into the duty-room, a tiny office with binoculars hanging from pegs, and waterproofs, gumboots, dog-harness and other gear stacked round the walls. There were a couple of deal chairs and a table covered with a large-scale map of the Forest of St Germain. This had been marked off into pencilled squares. The handler made a gesture over the map. 'Our dogs covered it all, Monsieur. There is nothing there.'

'Do you mean to say they didn't check once?'

The handler scratched his head. 'We had trouble with a bit of game, Monsieur. There was a hare or two. A couple of foxes' earths. We had quite a time getting them away from a clearing near the Carrefour Royal. They probably still smelled the gipsies.'

'Oh.' Bond was only mildly interested. 'Show me. Who were these gipsies?'

The handler pointed daintily with a grimy little

finger. 'These are the names from the old days. Here is the Etoile Parfaite, and here, where the killing took place, is the Carrefour des Curieux. And here, forming the bottom of the triangle, is the Carrefour Royal. It makes,' he added dramatically, 'a cross with the road of death.' He took a pencil out of his pocket and made a dot just off the crossroads. 'And this is the clearing, Monsieur. There was a gipsy caravan there for most of the winter. They left last month. Cleaned the place up all right, but, for the dogs, their scent will hang about there for months.'

Bond thanked him, and after inspecting and admiring the dogs and making some small talk about the handler's profession, he got into the Peugeot and went off to the gendarmerie in St Germain. 'Yes, certainly they had known the gipsies. Real Romany-looking fellows. Hardly spoke a word of French, but they had behaved themselves. There had been no complaints. Six men and two women. No. No one had seen them go. One morning they just weren't there any more. Might have been gone a week for all one knew. They had chosen an isolated spot.'

Bond took the D98 through the forest. When the great autoroute bridge showed up a quarter of a mile ahead over the road, Bond accelerated and then switched off the engine and coasted silently until he came to the

Carrefour Royal. He stopped and got out of the car without a sound, and, feeling rather foolish, softly entered the forest and walked with great circumspection towards where the clearing would be. Twenty vards inside the trees he came to it. He stood in the fringe of bushes and trees and examined it carefully. Then he walked in and went over it from end to end.

The clearing was about as big as two tennis courts and floored in thick grass and moss. There was one large patch of lilies of the valley and, under the bordering trees, a scattering of bluebells. To one side there was a low mound, perhaps a tumulus, completely surrounded and covered with brambles and brier roses now thickly in bloom. Bond walked round this and gazed in among the roots, but there was nothing to see except the earthy shape of the mound.

Bond took one last look round and then went to the corner of the clearing that would be nearest to the road. Here there was easy access through the trees. Were there traces of a path, a slight flattening of the leaves? Not more than would have been left by the gipsies or last year's picnickers. On the edge of the road there was a narrow passage between two trees. Casually Bond bent to examine the trunks. He stiffened and dropped to a crouch. With a fingernail, he delicately scraped away a narrow sliver of caked mud. It hid a deep scratch in the tree-trunk. He caught the scraps of mud in his free hand. He now spat and moistened the mud and carefully filled up the scratch again. There were three camouflaged scratches on one tree and four on the other. Bond walked quickly out of the trees on to the road. His car had stopped on a slight slope leading down under the autoroute bridge. Although there was some protection from the boom of the traffic on the autoroute, Bond pushed the car, jumped in and only engaged the gears when he was well under the bridge.

And now Bond was back in the clearing, above it, and he still did not know if his hunch had been right. It had been M's dictum that had put him on the scent – if it was a scent – and the mention of the gipsies. 'It was the gipsies the dogs smelled . . . Most of the winter . . . they went last month. No complaints . . . One morning they just weren't there any more.' The invisible factor. The invisible man. The people who are so much part of the background that you don't know if they're there or not. Six men and two girls and they hardly spoke a word of French. Good cover, gipsies. You could be a foreigner and yet not a foreigner, because you were only a gipsy. Some of them had gone off in the caravan. Had some of them stayed, built themselves a hide-out during the winter, a secret place from which the hijacking of the top secret dispatches had been the first sortie? Bond had thought he was building fantasies until he found the scratches, the carefully camouflaged scratches, on the two trees. They were just at the height where, if one was carrying any kind of a cycle, the pedals might catch against the bark. It could all be a pipedream, but it was good enough for Bond. The only question in his mind was whether these people had made a one-time-only coup or whether they were so confident of their security that they would try again. He confided only in Station F. Mary Ann Russell told him to be careful. Head of F, more constructively, ordered his unit at St Germain to cooperate. Bond said goodbye to Colonel Schreiber and moved to a camp bed in the unit's HQ – an anonymous house in an anonymous village backstreet. The unit had provided the camouflage outfit and the four Secret Service men who ran the unit had happily put themselves under Bond's orders. They realized as well as Bond did that if Bond managed to wipe the eye of the whole security machine of SHAPE, the Secret Service would have won a priceless feather in its cap *vis-à-vis* the SHAPE High Command, and M's worries over the independence of his unit would be gone for ever.

Bond, lying along the oak branch, smiled to himself.

Private armies, private wars. How much energy they siphoned off from the common cause, how much fire they directed away from the common enemy!

Six-thirty. Time for breakfast. Cautiously Bond's right hand fumbled in his clothing and came up to the slit of his mouth. Bond made the glucose tablet last as long as possible and then sucked another. His eyes never left the glade. The red squirrel that had appeared at first light and had been steadily eating away at young beech shoots ever since, ran a few feet nearer to the rose-bushes on the mound, picked up something and began turning it in his paws and nibbling at it. Two wood pigeons that had been noisily courting among the thick grass started to make clumsy, fluttering love. A pair of hedge sparrows went busily on collecting bits and pieces for a nest they were tardily building in a thorn-bush. The fat thrush finally located its worm and began pulling at it, its legs braced. Bees clustered thick among the roses on the mound, and from where he was, perhaps twenty yards away from and above the mound, Bond could just hear their summery sound. It was a scene from a fairytale – the roses, the lilies of the valley, the birds and the great shafts of sunlight lancing down through the tall trees into the pool of glistening green. Bond had climbed to his hide-out at four in the morning and he had never examined so closely or for so long the transition from night to a glorious day. He suddenly felt rather foolish. Any moment now and some damned bird would come and sit on his head!

It was the pigeons that gave the first alarm. With a loud clatter they took off and dashed into the trees. All the birds followed, and the squirrel. Now the glade was quiet except for the soft hum of the bees. What had sounded the alarm? Bond's heart began to thump. His eyes hunted, quartering the glade for a clue. Something was moving among the roses. It was a tiny movement, but an extraordinary one. Slowly, inch by inch, a single thorny stem, an unnaturally straight and rather thick one, was rising through the upper branches. It went on rising until it was a clear foot above the bush. Then it stopped. There was a solitary pink rose at the tip of the stem. Separated from the bush, it looked unnatural, but only if one happened to have watched the whole pro-cess. At a casual glance it was a stray stem and nothing else. Now, silently, the petals of the rose seemed to swivel and expand, the yellow pistils drew aside and sun glinted on a glass lens the size of a shilling. The lens seemed to be looking straight at Bond, but then very, very slowly, the rose-eye began to turn on its stem and continued to turn until the lens was again looking at Bond and the whole glade had been minutely surveyed. As if satisfied, the petals softly swivelled to cover the eye and very slowly the single rose descended to join the others.

Bond's breath came out with a rush. He momentarily closed his eyes to rest them. Gipsies! If that piece of machinery was any evidence, inside the mound, deep down in the earth, was certainly the most professional left-behind spy unit that had ever been devised – far more brilliant than anything England had prepared to operate in the wake of a successful German invasion, far better than what the Germans themselves had left behind in the Ardennes. A shiver of excitement and anticipation – almost of fear – ran down Bond's spine. So he had been right! But what was to be the next act?

Now, from the direction of the mound, came a thin high-pitched whine – the sound of an electric motor at very high revs. The rose bush trembled slightly. The bees took off, hovered, and settled again. Slowly, a jagged fissure formed down the centre of the big bush and smoothly widened. Now the two halves of the bush were opening like double doors. The dark aperture broadened until Bond could see the roots of the bush running into the earth on both sides of the opening doorway. The whine of machinery was louder and there was a glint of metal from the edges of the curved doors. It was like the opening of a hinged Easter egg. In a moment the two segments stood apart and the two halves of the rose bush, still alive with bees, were splayed widely open. Now the inside of the metal caisson that supported the earth and the roots of the bush were naked to the sun. There was a glint of pale electric light from the dark aperture between the curved doors. The whine of the motor had stopped. A head and shoulders appeared, and then the rest of the man. He climbed softly out and crouched, looking sharply round the glade. There was a gun – a Luger – in his hand. Satisfied, he turned and gestured into the shaft. The head and shoulders of a second man appeared. He handed up three pairs of what looked like snowshoes and ducked out of sight. The first man selected a pair and knelt and strapped them over his boots. Now he moved about more freely, leaving no footprints, for the grass flattened only momentarily under the wide mesh and then rose slowly again. Bond smiled to himself. Clever bastards!

The second man emerged. He was followed by a third. Between them they manhandled a motor-cycle out of the shaft and stood holding it slung between them by harness webbing while the first man, who was clearly the leader, knelt and strapped the snowshoes under their boots. Then, in single file, they moved off through the trees towards the road. There was something extraordinarily sinister about the way they softly high-stepped along through the shadows, lifting and carefully placing each big webbed foot in turn.

Bond let out a long sigh of released tension and laid his head softly down on the branch to relax the strain in his neck muscles. So that was the score! Even the last small detail could now be added to the file. While the two underlings were dressed in grey overalls, the leader was wearing the uniform of the Royal Corps of Signals and his motor-cycle was an olive green BSA M20 with a British Army registration number on its petrol tank. No wonder the SHAPE dispatch-rider had let him get within range. And what did the unit do with its top secret booty? Probably radioed the cream of it out at night. Instead of the periscope, a rose-stalk aerial would rise up from the bush, the pedal generator would get going deep down under the earth and off would go the high-speed cipher groups. Ciphers? There would be many good enemy secrets down that shaft if Bond could round up the unit when it was outside the hide-out. And what a chance to feed back phoney intelligence to GRU, the Soviet Military Intelligence Apparat which was presumably the control! Bond's thoughts raced.

The two underlings were coming back. They went into the shaft and the rose bush closed over it. The leader with his machine would be among the bushes on the verge of the road. Bond glanced at his watch.

Six-fifty-five. Of course! He would be waiting to see if a dispatch-rider came along. Either he did not know the man he had killed was doing a weekly run, which was unlikely, or he was assuming that SHAPE would now change the routine for additional security. These were careful people. Probably their orders were to clean up as much as possible before the summer came and there were too many holidaymakers about in the forest. Then the unit might be pulled out and put back again in the winter. Who could say what the long-term plans were? Sufficient that the leader was preparing for another kill.

The minutes ticked by. At seven-ten the leader reappeared. He stood in the shadow of a big tree at the edge of the clearing and whistled once on a brief, high, birdlike note. Immediately the rose bush began to open and the two underlings came out and followed the leader back into the trees. In two minutes they were back with the motor-cycle slung between them. The leader, after a careful look round to see that they had left no traces, followed them down into the shaft and the two halves of the rose bush closed swiftly behind him.

Half an hour later life had started up in the glade again. An hour later still, when the high sun had darkened the shadows, James Bond silently edged backwards along his branch, dropped softly on to a patch of moss behind some brambles and melted carefully back into the forest.

That evening Bond's routine call with Mary Ann Russell was a stormy one. She said: 'You're crazy. I'm not going to let you do it. I'm going to get Head of F to ring up Colonel Schreiber and tell him the whole story. This is SHAPE's job. Not yours.'

Bond said sharply: 'You'll do nothing of the sort. Colonel Schreiber says he's perfectly happy to let me make a dummy run tomorrow morning instead of the duty dispatch-rider. That's all he needs to know at this stage. Reconstruction of the crime sort of thing. He couldn't care less. He's practically closed the file on this business. Now, be a good girl and do as you're told. Just put my report on the printer to M. He'll see the point of me cleaning this thing up. He won't object.'

'Damn M! Damn you! Damn the whole silly Service!' There were angry tears in the voice. 'You're just a lot of children playing at Red Indians. Taking these people on by yourself! It's – it's showing off. That's all it is. Showing off.'

Bond was beginning to get annoyed. He said: 'That's enough, Mary Ann. Put that report on the printer. I'm sorry, but it's an order.'

There was resignation in the voice. 'Oh, all right.

You don't have to pull your rank on me. But don't get hurt. At least you'll have the boys from the local Station to pick up the bits. Good luck.'

'Thanks, Mary Ann. And will you have dinner with me tomorrow night? Some place like Armenonville. Pink champagne and gipsy violins. Paris in the spring routine.'

'Yes,' she said seriously. 'I'd like that. But then take care all the more, would you? Please?'

'Of course I will. Don't worry. Goodnight.'

''Night.'

Bond spent the rest of the evening putting a last high polish on his plans and giving a final briefing to the four men from the Station.

It was another beautiful day. Bond, sitting comfortably astride the throbbing BSA waiting for the off, could hardly believe in the ambush that would now be waiting for him just beyond the Carrefour Royal. The corporal from the Signal Corps who had handed him his empty dispatch-case and was about to give him the signal to go said: 'You look as if you'd been in the Royal Corps all your life, sir. Time for a haircut soon, I'd say, but the uniform's bang on. How d'you like the bike, sir?'

'Goes like a dream. I'd forgotten what fun these damned things are.'

'Give me a nice little Austin A40 any day, sir.' The

corporal looked at his watch. 'Seven o'clock just coming up.' He held up his thumb. 'Okay.'

Bond pulled the goggles down over his eyes, lifted a hand to the corporal, kicked the machine into gear and wheeled off across the gravel and through the main gates.

Off 184 and on to 307, through Bailly and Noisy-le-Roi and there was the straggle of St Nom. Here he would be turning sharp right on to D98 – the 'route de la mort', as the handler had called it. Bond pulled into the grass verge and once more looked to the long-barrel .45 Colt. He put the warm gun back against his stomach and left the jacket button undone. On your marks! Get set . . . !

Bond took the sharp corner and accelerated up to fifty. The viaduct carrying the Paris autoroute loomed up ahead. The dark mouth of the tunnel beneath it opened and swallowed him. The noise of his exhaust was gigantic, and for an instant there was a tunnel smell of cold and damp. Then he was out in the sunshine again and immediately across the Carrefour Royal. Ahead the oily tarmac glittered dead straight for two miles through the enchanted forest and there was a sweet smell of leaves and dew. Bond cut his speed to forty. The driving-mirror by his left hand shivered slightly with his speed. It showed nothing but an empty unfurling vista of road between lines of trees that curled away behind him like a green wake. No sign of the killer. Had he taken fright? Had there been some hitch? But then there was a tiny black speck in the centre of the convex glass – a midge that became a fly and then a bee and then a beetle. Now it was a crash helmet bent low over handlebars between two big black paws. God, he was coming fast! Bond's eyes flickered from the mirror to the road ahead and back to the mirror. When the killer's right hand went for his gun . . . !

Bond slowed – thirty-five, thirty, twenty. Ahead the tarmac was smooth as metal. A last quick look in the mirror. The right hand had left the handlebars. The sun on the man's goggles made huge fiery eyes below the rim of the crash helmet. Now! Bond braked fiercely and skidded the BSA through forty-five degrees, killing the engine. He was not quite quick enough on the draw. The killer's gun flared twice and a bullet tore into the saddle-springs beside Bond's thigh. But then the Colt spoke its single word, and the killer and his BSA, as if lassoed from within the forest, veered crazily off the road, leapt the ditch and crashed head-on into the trunk of a beech. For a moment the tangle of man and machinery clung to the broad trunk and then, with a metallic death-rattle, toppled backwards into the grass.

Bond got off his machine and walked over to the ugly twist of khaki and smoking steel. There was no need to feel for a pulse. Wherever the bullet had struck, the crash helmet had smashed like an eggshell. Bond turned away and thrust his gun back into the front of his tunic. He had been lucky. It would not do to press his luck. He got on the BSA and accelerated back down the road.

He leant the BSA up against one of the scarred trees just inside the forest and walked softly through to the edge of the clearing. He took up his stand in the shadow of the big beech. He moistened his lips and gave, as near as he could, the killer's bird-whistle. He waited. Had he got the whistle wrong? But then the bush trembled and the high thin whine began. Bond hooked his right thumb through his belt within inches of his gun-butt. He hoped he would not have to do any more killing. The two underlings had not seemed to be armed. With any luck they would come quietly.

Now the curved doors were open. From where he was, Bond could not see down the shaft, but within seconds the first man was out and putting on his snowshoes and the second followed. Snowshoes! Bond's heart missed a beat. He had forgotten them! They must be hidden back there in the bushes. Blasted fool! Would they notice?

The two men came slowly towards him, delicately placing their feet. When he was about twenty feet away, the leading man said something softly in what sounded like Russian. When Bond did not reply, the two men stopped in their tracks. They stared at him in astonishment, waiting perhaps for the answer to a password. Bond sensed trouble. He whipped out his gun and moved towards them, crouching. 'Hands up.' He gestured with the muzzle of the Colt. The leading man shouted an order and threw himself forward. At the same time the second man made a dash back towards the hideout. A rifle boomed from among the trees and the man's right leg buckled under him. The men from the Station broke cover and came running. Bond fell to one knee and clubbed upwards with his gun-barrel at the hurtling body. It made contact but then the man was on him. Bond saw fingernails flashing towards his eyes, ducked and ran into an uppercut. Now a hand was at his right wrist and his gun was being slowly turned on him. Not wanting to kill, he had kept the safety catch up. He tried to get his thumb to it. A boot hit him in the side of the head and he let the gun go and fell back. Through a red mist he saw the muzzle of the gun pointing at his face. The thought flashed through his mind that he was going to die – die for showing mercy . . . !

Suddenly the gun muzzle had gone and the weight of the man was off him. Bond got to his knees and then to his feet. The body, spreadeagled in the grass beside him, gave a last kick. There were bloody rents in the back of the dungarees. Bond looked round. The four men from the Station were in a group. Bond undid the strap of his crash helmet and rubbed the side of his head. He said: 'Well, thanks. Who did it?'

Nobody answered. The men looked embarrassed.

Bond walked towards them, puzzled. 'What's up?'

Suddenly Bond caught a trace of movement behind the men. An extra leg showed – a woman's leg. Bond laughed out loud. The men grinned sheepishly and looked behind them. Mary Ann Russell, in a brown shirt and black jeans, came out from behind them with her hands up. One of the hands held what looked like a .22 target pistol. She brought her hands down and tucked the pistol into the top of her jeans. She came up to Bond. She said anxiously: 'You won't blame anybody, will you? I just wouldn't let them leave this morning without me.' Her eyes pleaded. 'Rather lucky I did come, really. I mean, I just happened to get to you first. No one wanted to shoot for fear of hitting you.'

Bond smiled into her eyes. He said: 'If you hadn't come, I'd have had to break that dinner date.' He turned back to the men, his voice businesslike. 'All right. One of you take the motor-bike and report the gist of this to Colonel Schreiber. Say we're waiting for his team before we take a look at the hideout. And would he include a couple of anti-sabotage men. That shaft may be booby-trapped. All right?'

Bond took the girl by the arm. He said: 'Come over here. I want to show you a bird's nest.'

'Is that an order?'

'Yes.'

a little history

Penguin Modern Classics were launched in 1961, and have been shaping the reading habits of generations ever since.

The list began with distinctive grey spines and evocative pictorial covers – a look that, after various incarnations, continues to influence their current design – and with books that are still considered landmark classics today.

Penguin Modern Classics have caused scandal and political change, inspired great films and broken down barriers, whether social, sexual or the boundaries of language itself. They remain the most provocative, groundbreaking, exciting and revolutionary works of the last 100 years (or so).

In 2011, on the fiftieth anniversary of the Modern Classics, we're publishing fifty Mini Modern Classics: the very best short fiction by writers ranging from Beckett to Conrad, Nabokov to Saki, Updike to Wodehouse. Though they don't take long to read, they'll stay with you long after you turn the final page.

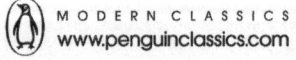

MODERN CLASSICS
www.penguinclassics.com